Can You Imagine?

Eldonna L. Evertts/*Language Arts*
Bernard J. Weiss/*Linguistics and Reading*

Susan B. Cruikshank/*Reading and Language Arts*

Educational Consultants
Jack P. Henderson
Janet Sprout

Related Satellite Books
Lyman C. Hunt /*General Editor*

**The Holt
Basic Reading
System**

Level 6
HOLT, RINEHART AND WINSTON, PUBLISHERS
New York · Toronto · London · Sydney

ISBN 0-03-016991-7
7890 071 98765432

Acknowledgments:

Grateful acknowledgment is given to the following authors and publishers:

Doubleday & Company, Inc., for "Conversation," from *Fifty-One New Nursery Rhymes*, by Rose Fyleman. Copyright 1932 by Doubleday & Company, Inc. Used by permission.

Harcourt Brace Jovanovich, Inc., for "Good Morning, Cat" from *Wide Awake and Other Poems*. Copyright © 1959 by Myra Cohn Livingston. Used by permission.

Lothrop, Lee & Shepard Co., Inc., for "A Good House," adapted from *The Mitten* by Alvin Tresselt. Copyright © 1964 by Lothrop, Lee & Shepard Co., Inc. Used by permission.

Western Publishing Company, for "A Bear's Life" by Orissa Rines from *Story Parade* Magazine. Copyright 1953 by Story Parade, Inc. Used by permission.

Art Credits:

Tim and Greg Hildebrandt, pages 4–13
Ray Cruz, pages 14–15, 51
Aaron Heller, pages 16–25
Lorraine Fox, pages 26–32, 42
Marilyn Bass Goldman, page 33
Karl W. Stücklen, pages 34–41
Gilbert Riswold, pages 43–50
Jack Endewelt, pages 52–59
David K. Stone, pages 60–61 (copied)
Diane de Groat, pages 62–63

Cover design by Pellegrini, Kaestle & Gross, Inc.

Table of Contents

A Good House

A mouse saw a blue mitten.

He ran up to it.

"What a good house for a mouse,"
he said.

And in he went.

A little frog saw the mitten.

He ran up to it.

"What a good house for a frog,"
he said.

"Come in," said the mouse.

"You will love it in here."

And in went the frog.

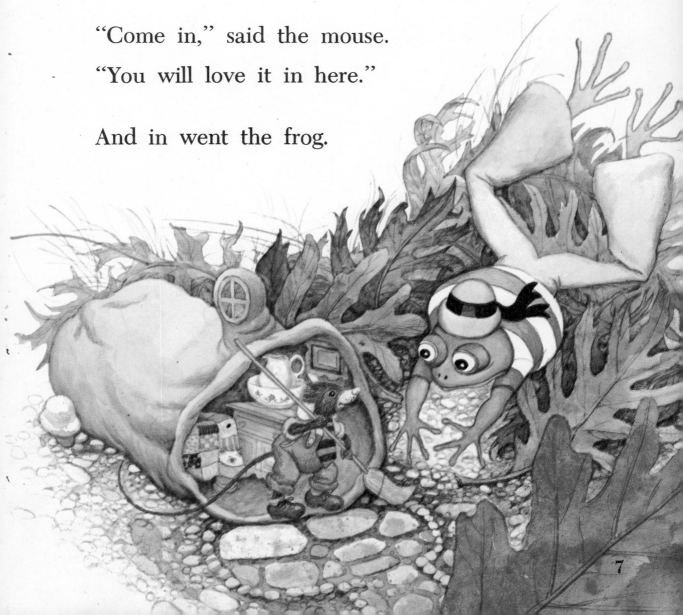

A pig saw the blue mitten.

He ran up to it.

"What a good house for a pig,"
he said.

"Come in," said the mouse again.

In went the pig with the mouse
and the frog.

A wolf ran up to the blue mitten.
"What a good house for a wolf,"
he said.

"Come in," said the mouse again.

In went the wolf with the mouse
and the frog and the pig.

A sheep saw the blue mitten.
"What a good house for a sheep,"
she said.

"Come in," said the mouse again.

In went the sheep with the mouse
and the frog and the pig and the wolf.

A bear saw the blue mitten.
"What a good house for a bear,"
he said.

"Come in," said the mouse again.

In went the bear with the mouse
and the frog and the pig and the wolf
and the sheep.

A bee saw the blue mitten.

"What a good house for a bee,"
he said.

"Can I come in with you?"

"No!" said the mouse.

"Stop!" said the frog.

In went the bee.

Pop went the mitten!

Out went the mouse and the frog

and the pig and the wolf

and the sheep and the bear

and the bee!

13

Conversation

"Mousie, mousie,
Where is your little wee housie?"

"Here is the door,
Under the floor,"
Said mousie, mousie.

"Mousie, mousie,
May I come into your housie?"

14

"You can't get in,
You have to be thin,"
Said mousie, mousie.

"Mousie, mousie,
Won't you come out
of your housie?"

"I'm sorry to say,
I'm busy all day,"
Said mousie, mousie.

—Rose Fyleman

City Mouse, Country Mouse

A city mouse came to the country.
He came to see the country mouse.

"Come in, come in,"
said the country mouse.
"It's good to see you.
You will like it here."

"What do you eat?"
asked the city mouse.

"Beans and water,"
said the country mouse.
"I will get some for you."

The city mouse didn't like beans.

He didn't like the little house.

He didn't like the country.

"Come with me to the city.

You will like it," said the city mouse.

The country mouse went
with the city mouse.
They came to the city.
They saw a big house.

"Here is my house,"
said the city mouse.
"Come in.
I will find some cookies to eat."

The city mouse went to find cookies.

He saw some good cookies.

"Come here," he said.

"Come and eat."

The country mouse ran to eat.

He did not get cookies in the country.

"What good cookies," he said.

A cat came into the house.
He saw the city mouse
and the country mouse.

The city mouse saw the cat.
"A cat!" he said.
And out he ran.

The country mouse ran out
with the city mouse.

"Good-by," said the country mouse.
"The city is not for me.
I like the big house.
I like the cookies.
But I do not like the cat."

The country mouse ran to his house.

He didn't go to the city again.

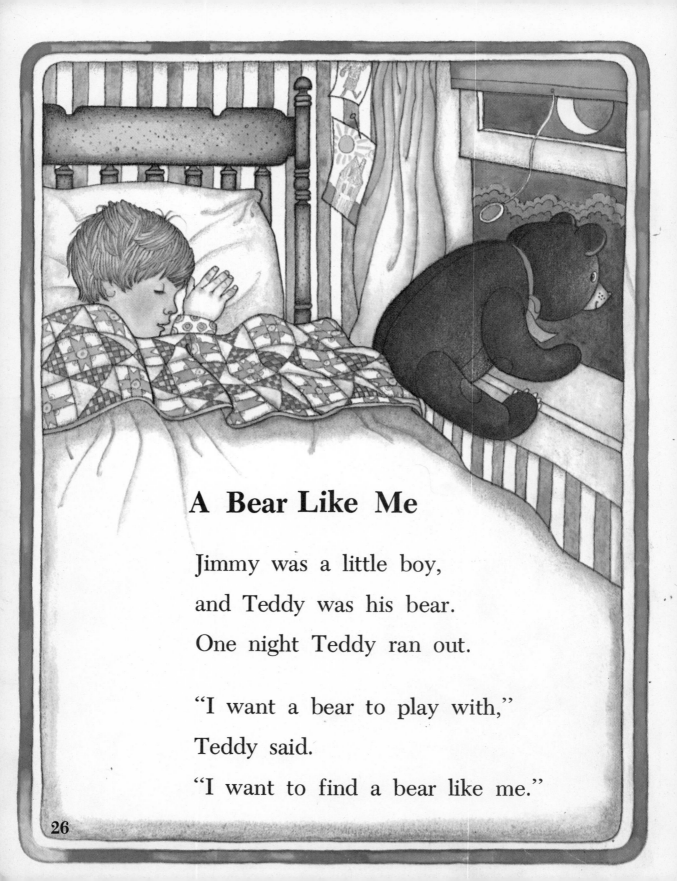

A Bear Like Me

Jimmy was a little boy,
and Teddy was his bear.
One night Teddy ran out.

"I want a bear to play with,"
Teddy said.
"I want to find a bear like me."

Teddy saw a little house.

The house was open.

Teddy went in.

He saw a dog.

"Hello," said Teddy.

"What do you want?" asked the dog.

"A bear like me," said Teddy.

"You won't find a bear in here!
  Good night!" said the dog.

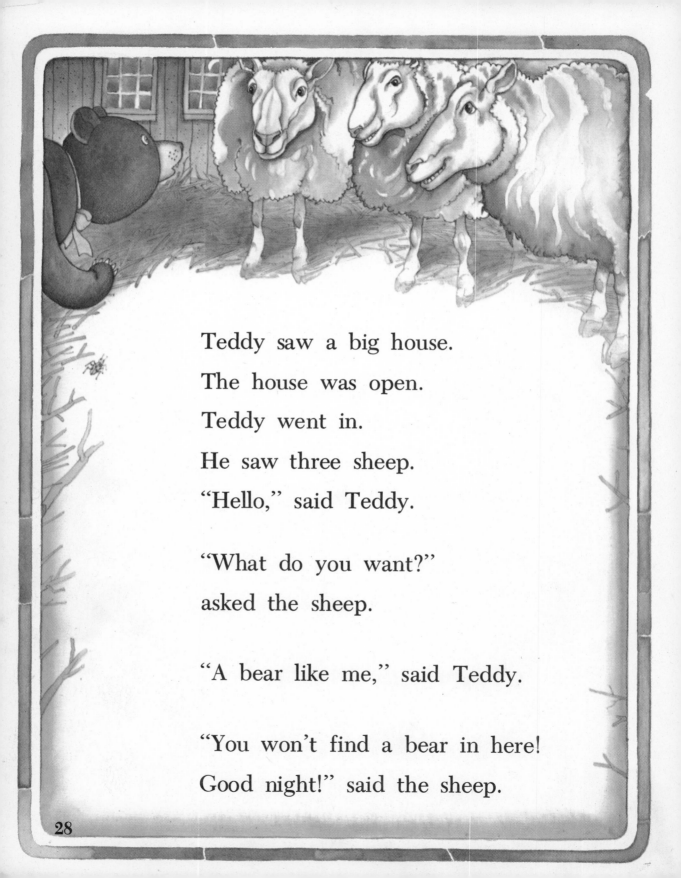

Teddy saw a big house.

The house was open.

Teddy went in.

He saw three sheep.

"Hello," said Teddy.

"What do you want?"
asked the sheep.

"A bear like me," said Teddy.

"You won't find a bear in here!
Good night!" said the sheep.

Teddy saw a cow.

"Hello," said Teddy.

"What do you want?" asked the cow.

"A bear like me," said Teddy.

"You won't find a bear in here.
Good night!" said the cow.

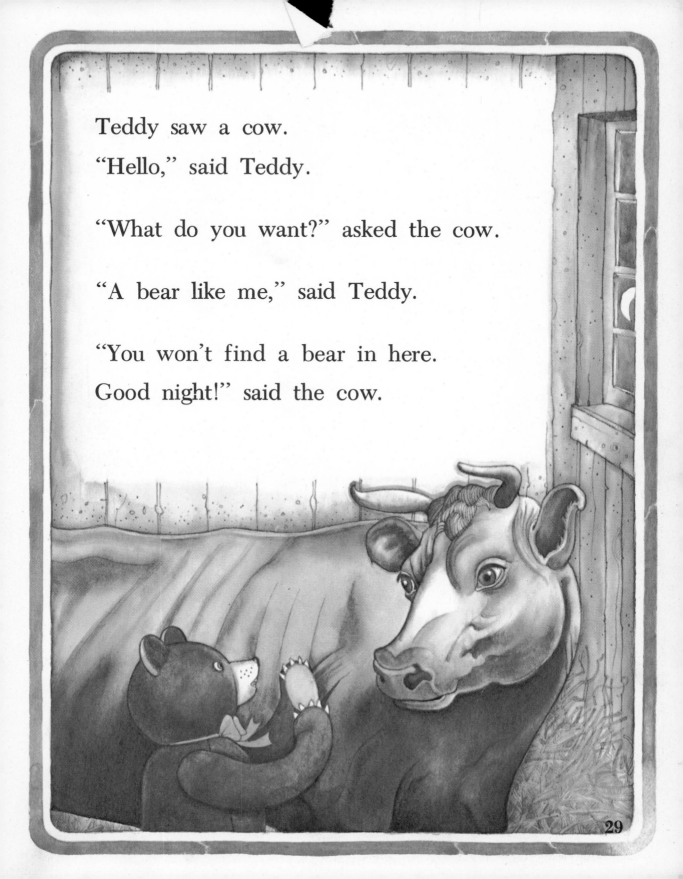

Teddy ran out.

He saw a bear.

It was a **big** bear!

It was not like Teddy.

"Stop," said the big bear.

"What do you want?"

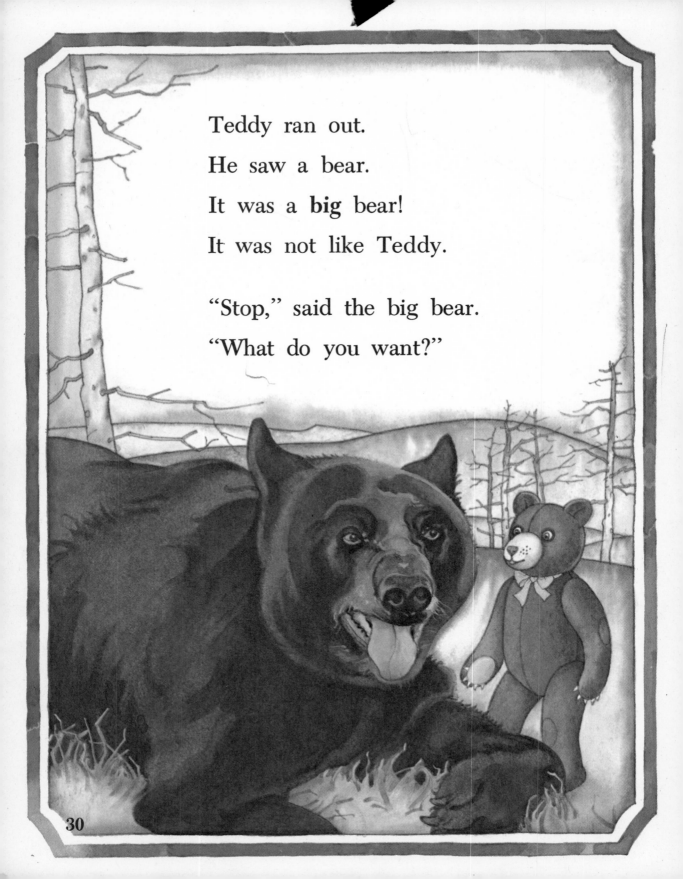

"I want to find a bear like me,"
said Teddy.
"You are a big bear.
You are not like me.
Good night and good-by!"

Teddy ran to Jimmy.

"I like to play with Jimmy," he said.
"Big bears are not like me!"

A Bear's Life

A Bear takes life quite easy
As a rule.
In Fall he just trots off to bed
Instead of school.

—Orissa Rines

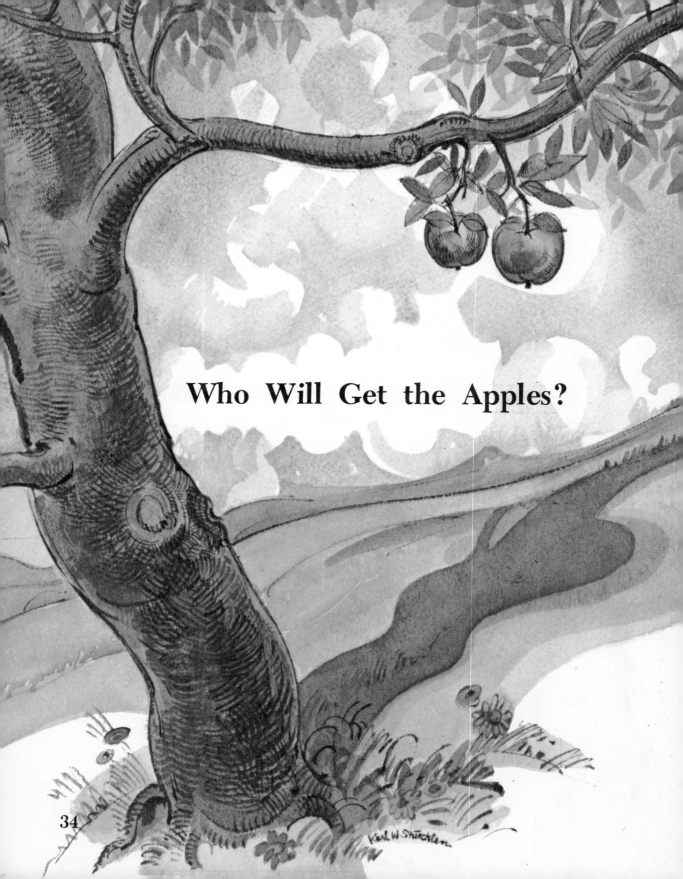

Who Will Get the Apples?

Two pigs saw a big apple tree.

"Do you see what I see?"
asked the big pig.

"Apples!" said the little pig.
"I see apples on the tree!"

"Two apples," said the big pig.
"One is for you, and one is for me."

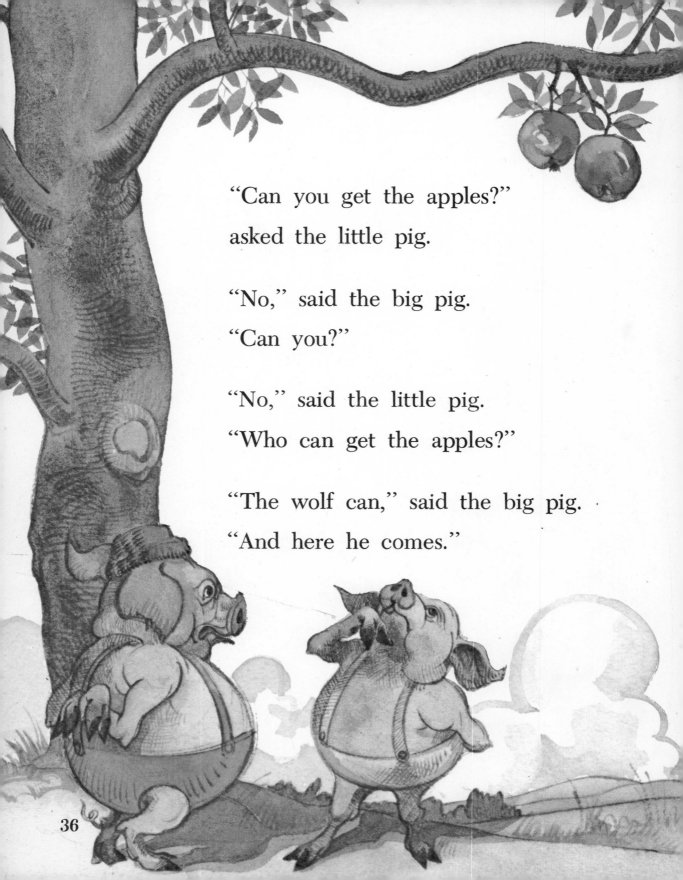

"Can you get the apples?"
asked the little pig.

"No," said the big pig.
"Can you?"

"No," said the little pig.
"Who can get the apples?"

"The wolf can," said the big pig.
"And here he comes."

"Wolf," said the big pig.
"Do you see the apples?
Will you get one for me
and one for my brother?"

"No," said the wolf.
"I won't get apples for you.
I will get apples for me."

The wolf went up the tree.

"I will trick the wolf,"
said the big pig to his brother.
"He won't eat the apples.
But you will see.
I will make the wolf get the apples
for you and me."

"Wolf," said the big pig.
"I can jump up and down.
Can you?" he asked.

"I can jump," said the wolf.
"See me?"

"I see you," said the big pig.

39

The wolf went up and down,
up and down,
up and down.

The apples went up and down,
up and down,
up and down,
down, down.

"What a good trick!"
said the little pig.
"Here come the apples!"

The wolf didn't see the pigs.

He didn't see the apples come down.

The pigs ran with the apples.

And the wolf went up and down,

    up and down,

        up and down.

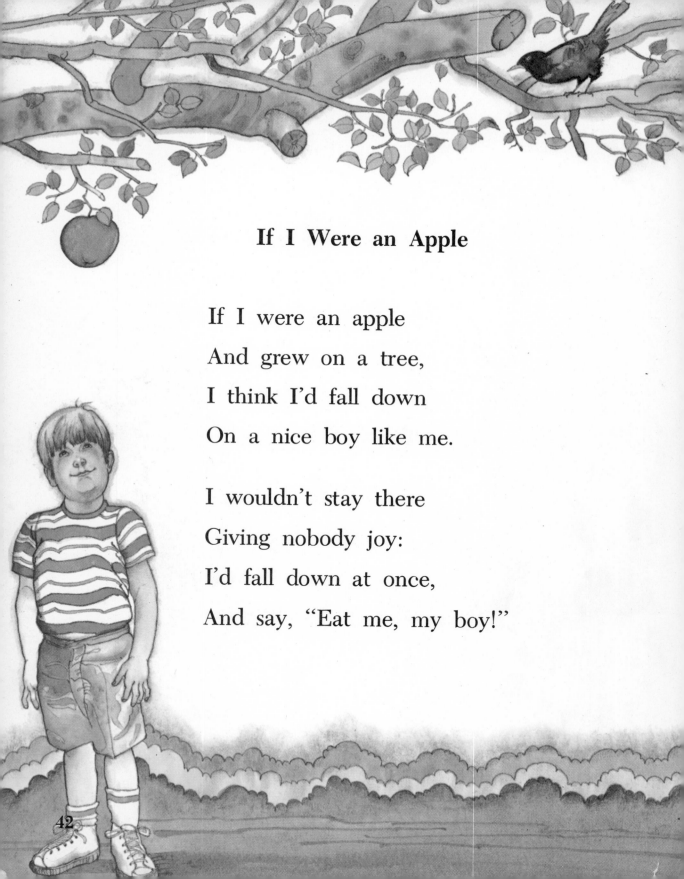

If I Were an Apple

If I were an apple
And grew on a tree,
I think I'd fall down
On a nice boy like me.

I wouldn't stay there
Giving nobody joy:
I'd fall down at once,
And say, "Eat me, my boy!"

Who Will Play?

"I want to play," said the cat.
"The little boy likes to play.
He will play with me."

The cat ran to the little boy.

44

"No, no, cat," said the little boy.
"I do not want to play with you.
I want to play with my game."

The cat ran out.

"The little sister likes to play,"
said the cat.
"She will play with me."

The cat ran up to the girl.

"No, no, cat," said the little sister.
"I do not want to play with you.
I want to read my book."

The cat ran to the mouse house.

"Mouse, mouse," said the cat.
"Come on out.
Come out and play with me."

"No," said the mouse.
"I do not play with cats."

The cat saw the goldfish in a bowl.
He ran to the bowl.

"Hello," said the cat.
"Will you play with me?"

"No," said the goldfish in the bowl.
"I do not play with cats."

"Who will play with me?"
asked the cat.

"I will," said the big dog.
He ran to the cat.

"I will play with the little boy,"
said the cat.
"I will play with his little sister.
I will play with the goldfish
and the mouse.
But I will **not** play with a dog!"

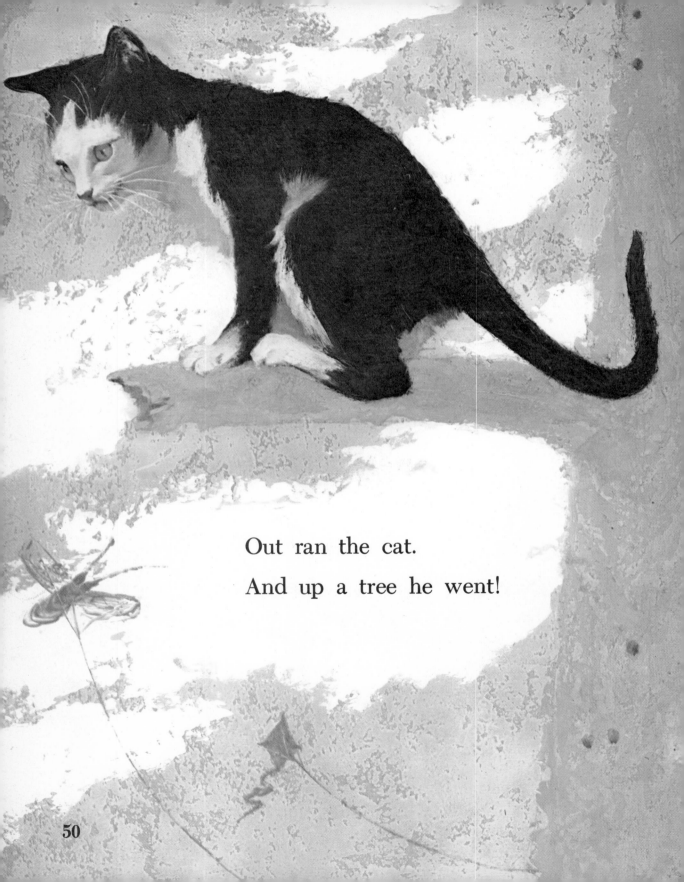

Out ran the cat.

And up a tree he went!

Good Morning, Cat

Good morning, cat,
you're in my yard
and sniffing for a mouse;
you might as well give up — because
he's hiding in the house.

—Myra Cohn Livingston

The Big City

A burro went down a country road.
She saw a frog in the road.

"Little frog," said the burro.
"I want to go to the city.
I want to see people and stores.
I want to see cars and big houses.
Where is the city?"

"Here is a sign," said the frog.

"It tells where to go.

Can you read it?"

"No!" said the burro.

"I will read the sign for you,"
said the frog.
"It says, 'To the City.'
Go down the road.
You will find the city."

The burro went down the road.

She saw a sign.

And she saw three sheep.

"Who can read the sign?"
asked the burro.
"I want to find the city."

"I can read the sign,"
said the big sheep.
"It says, 'To the City.'
Go down the road,
and you will find the city."

The burro went down the road.

She didn't see the city.

She saw a big sign.

"Where is the city?"
she asked a cow.
"Can you read the sign for me?"

"The sign says, 'City.'
You are in the city," said the cow.

"The city!" said the burro.

"Where are the cars and people?

Where are the houses and stores?"

"Go down the road," said the cow.

"And you will see the big city."

The burro went down the road.

What did the burro see?

She did not see the city!

But she did see a sign.

"The frog can't read," said the burro.

"The big sheep can't read.

And the cow can't read."

"Who can read?" asked the burro.

"Who can read the sign?

Can someone read the sign for me?"

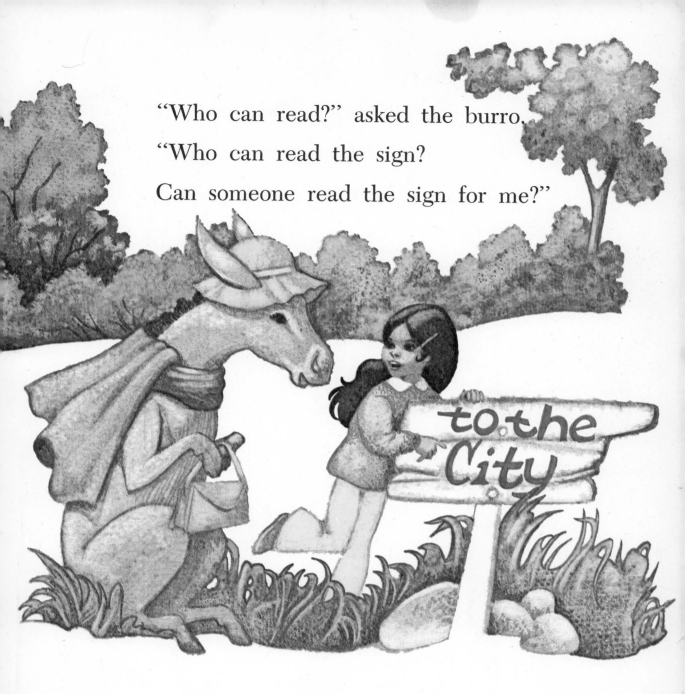

A little girl came out from the store.

"I can read!" said the girl.

"I can read the sign for you."

Stringing Words

Big   apples   are   here.

blue
good
big
little

apples	Jimmy
cat	I
brother	you
houses	city
house	tree

	the	a	some	one
no	where	for	into	in

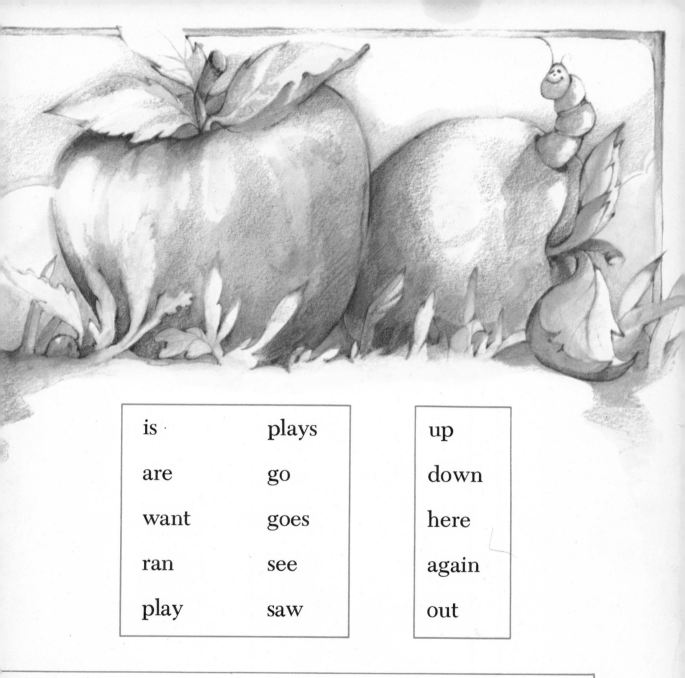

is	plays
are	go
want	goes
ran	see
play	saw

up
down
here
again
out

two	three	who	what
to	with	and	not

New Words

The words listed beside the page numbers below are intro-duced in *Can You Imagine?*, Level 6 in THE HOLT BASIC READING SYSTEM.

6. mouse	eat	tree
mitten	22. cat	39. jump
7. frog	26. Jimmy	47. cats
11. bear	Teddy	48. bowl
12. bee	night	53. road
pop	27. open	stores
16. city	hello	cars
country	34. apples	houses
18. beans	35. apple	60. can't